Tinderbox

Written by Hans Christian Andersen

Retold by Penny Dolan

Illustrated by Javier Joaquin

Collins

Chapter 1

One, two! One, two! Jack marched along the road. His soldier's coat was tattered and worn, and his boots were full of holes, but his smile was cheerful and bright. The wars were over and the armies sent home, but Jack had no home to welcome him. So all he could do was keep walking and whistling along the dusty road, hoping to meet good fortune.

An odd, twisted tree grew by the roadside, and under its shadows waited an old woman.

"Good day," Jack said, politely.

She cackled and pointed a bony finger at him. "I've a job for you, soldier boy."

"What sort of job?" Jack asked.

"One for the brave," she answered.

"I can be brave, if it's worth my while," he told her, grinning.

"I guessed that as soon as I saw your handsome face," she said. "Come and look at this!"

Within the hollow tree trunk was a narrow tunnel. Jack felt curious.

"If you dare go down there, right under the earth," the woman said, "you'll become a rich man."

As Jack only had a penny in his pocket, and an empty knapsack, he was delighted by these words. "Tell me more, kind lady," he begged.

"Down there, lit by magical candles, are three great caverns. Each one contains a chest of money. Once you're down there, you can gather as many coins as you desire."

"How will I get down?" Jack asked.

"That's simple," she answered, showing him a thick rope tied round a sturdy branch. "I'll lower you."

"But how will I get out again?" Jack asked.

"Oh, that?" she said, rather impatiently. "Shout when you're done and I'll haul you up."

She looked quite strong so Jack nodded. "I'll do it."

To his surprise, the woman took off her blue and white apron and handed it to him.

"You'll need this, soldier. Each chest is guarded by a dog, but don't worry. As soon as you spread this apron before them, the dogs will do you no harm."

Jack was puzzled. "Good woman, this is kindness indeed. What do you need in return?"

The woman sighed. "Ah me! All I want is my granny's old tinderbox. How many nights did she use it to light her fire?" She dabbed tears from her eyes. "Alas! It got left below years ago. Now I'm too old to clamber down and it's worthless to anyone else. Just get me the tinderbox, soldier, and I'll be content."

So Jack climbed inside the hollow tree.
He lowered himself down the tunnel,
his heart echoing in the darkness.

Chapter 2

After a while, Jack stood in a cave. The walls were covered in candles and in the middle stood a chest of money. However, the dog guarding the lid was unlike any that Jack had ever seen. Its eyes were as large and round as saucers. The dog looked at Jack and gave a low growl.

Jack dared not show fear. "Hello, handsome," he said, spreading the blue apron on the ground. "Sit!" At once, the dog jumped down and sat on the cloth, perfectly still. "Good boy!" Jack said, thankfully.

The chest was full of copper coins. "Copper's good, but what'll come next?" Jack wondered.

Taking a pocketful of copper coins, he told the dog to jump back on the box, picked up the apron and walked deeper into the tunnel.

As Jack entered the next cave, he heard ferocious growls. An even larger dog crouched on the second chest. It watched him with eyes the size of serving dishes, as if waiting for the moment to spring.

Jack didn't dare show his fear. The creature, no matter how odd or ugly, was still just a dog. So Jack spread out the blue apron.

"Hello, handsome," he said again, and pointed at the apron. "Sit, boy, sit!" At once, the strange creature jumped down and sat there, wagging its tail. Jack was so glad he almost wished he had a tail to wag too.

The second chest was full of silver coins so Jack put a few handfuls in his other pocket, saying, "Silver's better, but I wonder what'll come next?"

He shut the lid, patted the dog's head and it jumped back into place, just as before. "Stay!" Jack said firmly, making sure the animal didn't follow him.

When Jack entered the third cave, his own eyes almost popped out of his head. This dog had eyes the size of cartwheels. They glared and stared at Jack like two enormous round lanterns. The creature was almost as big as a horse, its paws were the size of doorsteps and when it growled, the rocks almost shook.

Jack needed all his courage to bend down and spread out the apron. To his delight, the dog jumped down just as obediently as the others had done.

"Good boy! Just you sit there comfortably," said Jack, lifting the lid. This last chest was full of bright golden coins. "And gold is best of all," he said, laughing, as he filled his knapsack full.

Then Jack remembered the old woman's request.
He soon found the rusty tinderbox, resting on a ledge of rock.

"Why does she want this dirty thing?" he wondered.
"Surely money's more useful?"

Jack went back to the tunnel and shouted up. At once the woman's face appeared. "You took a long time! Were you snoozing down there, you lazy lump?" she said angrily.

As she hauled him up, he saw her smile was not as kind as before and she had a sly look to her face. She put on a pitiful voice. "Give me my tinderbox, soldier," she wheedled. "Stretch out your arm and hand it to me now."

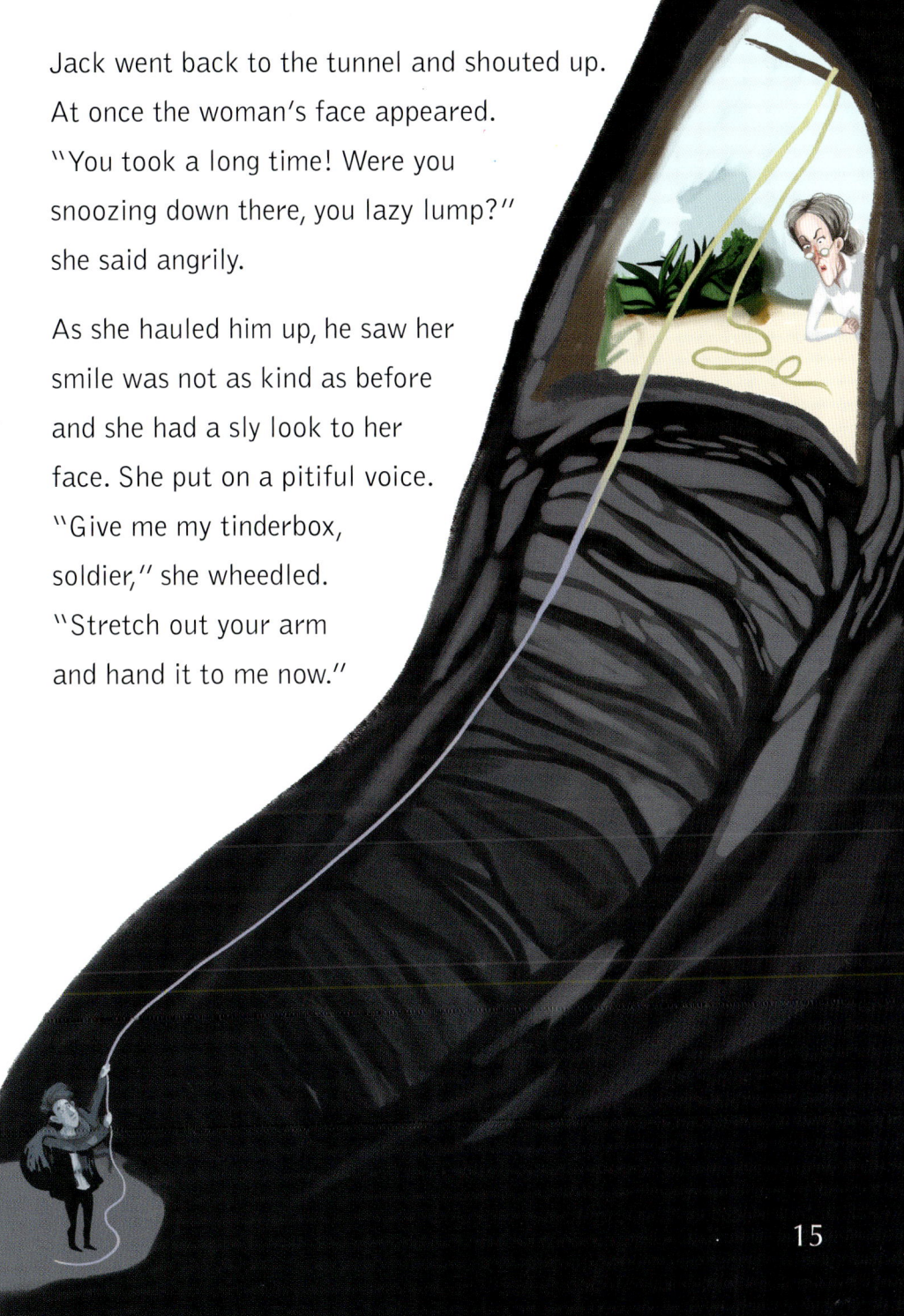

Jack suddenly realised that, once she had her precious tinderbox, she'd let the rope slip and he'd be left in the caves below. He shook his head.

"Give it to me, idiot!" she screeched, her face screwed up with hate.

"No, I won't!" Jack yelled. Using the last of his strength, he scrambled up and out of the dreadful tree, and tumbled onto the fresh green grass.

"Give me my box!" she screamed, snatching and scratching at him.

Jack looked at her coldly. "No," he told her. "You would've left me to die. I'm keeping the tinderbox myself."

By now, the old woman was so full of fury that she burst into a cloud of dust and ashes.

"That's you gone," said Jack, and set off down the road again, glad to be alive.

Chapter 3

Before long, Jack reached a very grand city with houses and shops and churches, and the king's palace towering above.

Now Jack had money, he could enjoy himself. He booked a grand set of rooms, bought fashionable clothes and ate in the best restaurants, just like a real gentleman. Yet, as he went about the city, Jack still shared his money with the poor, especially the children begging on the street corners.

Jack's wealth brought many new friends. Night after night, they gathered around, helping him to idle his days away and spend all his money on feasts and games.

However, a day came when Jack found his money spent and his false friends gone. Sitting alone and shivering in a wretched attic room, Jack thought how foolish he'd been. He wrapped his soldier's coat round himself, just to keep warm, and out of the pocket tumbled the tinderbox. Jack rubbed the rusty object one time, remembering the chests of coins. How he wished he had money now!

Immediately, in a burst of light, the dog with saucer eyes appeared. Jack backed away, alarmed, but then he saw the dog's tail was wagging. The creature was happy to see him! It carried a purse of copper coins in its mouth, which it dropped at Jack's feet.

"Good boy!" Jack said, praising the strange animal. "No wonder the hag wanted this tinderbox for herself."

Then Jack remembered the other two dogs. He rubbed the tinderbox twice and wished. There was another flash of light and the second dog appeared. Its two eyes – the size of serving dishes – looked eagerly at Jack. Proudly, it dropped a purse full of silver at his feet.

"Thank you," said Jack, and the dog sat there happily.

Finally, Jack took a deep breath and summoned the third dog, the one with cartwheel eyes. This time, in a blaze of light, the huge hound appeared, almost filling the attic.
Jack could barely say a word, but speak he must. "Well done! You good boy!" he cried. Immediately, the dog wagged its tail and dropped its purse of gold before Jack.

Once Jack was over the shock, he ruffled their ears and patted their backs and told them all they were clever dogs.

Then, in a flash, they vanished – but the money remained.

This time, Jack paid all he owed, shared some with the poor and lived wisely all winter. If ever he needed more money, he summoned the strange dogs.

Chapter 4

When spring came, the king and queen drove in procession through the city, along with all the lords and ladies. The king wanted the people to see him and admire his costly robes and glittering jewels. He wanted people to gaze at his glass carriage where the queen sat in silks and satin. Needless to say, this procession brought little joy to the hungry people of the city.

However, the one person the king did *not* want anyone to see was his daughter, the princess, who he kept in a tall copper tower. She had to ride in a copper coach without any windows.

Jack soon heard the story: when the princess was born, her nurse dreamt that she'd marry a common soldier. This so horrified the king and queen that they'd kept their precious daughter hidden away ever since. Even so, the servants whispered that the princess was as bright and lovely as a fine summer's day.

As Jack saw the grim copper carriage pass by, he felt sorry for the lonely princess trapped inside. Despite all her riches, her life must be very sad. So, come midnight, he took out the tinderbox and summoned the dog with the cartwheel eyes.

"My wish this time," Jack told the creature, "isn't for coins, but for you to go to the palace, find the princess and secretly bring her here."

In moments, the enormous dog returned with the princess fast asleep on its back. As soon as she opened her eyes, Jack bowed and spoke softly. "Good evening, Princess," he began. "Please don't be afraid. We mean you no harm."

"Oh!" she gasped, sitting up quickly. She looked about her and smiled. The princess felt happy to see Jack's friendly face and to be somewhere that wasn't her own dull room. She was fascinated by Jack's strange dog too. "What an interesting animal," she said, stroking its rough fur, "and what magnificent eyes!"

So Jack and the princess spent many hours talking and dancing. Just before dawn, the wheel-eyed dog carried her safely back to the palace. When the princess woke, she decided she'd had a wonderful dream.

The next night, the dog brought the princess to Jack again and they were even happier. She loved hearing about Jack's adventures, he loved her kind heart and cheerful laugh, and the great dog took her safely back, just as before.

Chapter 5

When the queen saw the princess yawning and smiling to herself, she grew suspicious. The queen didn't believe in this mysterious dream. So she quietly summoned her nimblest maid.

"I don't trust this tale," she said. "Tonight, put on your best running slippers and follow the princess wherever she goes. Mark any door she enters with this chalk." It was a cunning plan.

However, the enormous dog had good ears as well as good eyes and that night, he heard the swift footsteps following them. As the princess slipped through Jack's door, the dog hid in the shadows.

The queen's maid arrived in time to hear Jack's door rattle shut. She drew a large cross on the door. "Now the guards will get you," she sneered. She threw the chalk on the ground and ran swiftly off towards the palace.

The clever dog seized the chalk and speedily drew a cross on every door in that area of the city. Very soon, the guards arrived, holding their lanterns high, searching for the marked door.

"Here's a cross!" shouted a guard.

"No, it's this door!" shouted another.

"Or this?" asked the others, puzzled.

It was impossible to discover which door the princess had entered.

Chapter 6

The queen was extremely displeased by this, but she didn't give up. When the next evening came, she hung a small silk bag around the princess's neck.

"You must wear this, dear daughter," she said. "The herbs inside will keep away any dark dreams."

The queen hadn't filled the bag with lavender and sweet herbs but with tiny, hard seeds. As she leant over her daughter's bed, she secretly snipped a tiny hole in the corner of the bag. "Good night, my dear."

At midnight, as the princess rode through the city on the enormous dog, the tiny seeds fell out, marking a path straight to Jack's door. The seeds were too tiny for the dog to spot, and Jack and the princess only had eyes for each other, so the queen's cunning plan worked.

Soon after daybreak, the guards burst in through Jack's door. They dragged him from his rooms and through the streets to the palace, and flung him in the dungeon below the bell tower.

"The king will sentence you at noon, soldier," the captain of the guards told Jack. "Those happy hours dancing with the princess will cost you your life."

Chapter 7

Jack didn't regret dancing with the princess, yet how terrible it felt to be in prison, awaiting his own death. How he wished the tinderbox was with him now, when he needed it most. If only he'd had time to snatch it up, he'd be saved.

Nine ... ten ... each time the bell struck, Jack trembled. What could he do? His hands were sweating and he felt sick. There was a tightness in the middle of his stomach. Already, the crowds were starting to fill the courtyard.

Then, as Jack peered through the narrow bars, he saw a small boy begging scraps from the palace kitchen. Could this be his way out?

Jack whistled, calling the little lad over. "Will you do something for me?" he asked, hopefully.

"Of course, sir!" the boy answered, because the friendly soldier had bought him suppers in the past.

Jack smiled. "Run to my rooms faster than the wind, child. Bring me the tinderbox you'll find on the table. Please hurry, and if you're in time, you'll be well rewarded. If not, you'll have my thanks."

As the boy raced away, Jack heard royal drums and trumpets. Before long, the lords and ladies entered the courtyard, followed by the king and queen, parading in all their finery. Was this it? Was Jack out of time?

The captain of the guards unlocked the prison gates and marched Jack across to face the king. Jack stood there boldly, trying not to tremble at the sight of the executioner's axe.

The crowd were afraid for Jack, too. They wondered what would become of the good-hearted soldier who'd shared his fortune during the winter's cold.

The king had a cruel smile on his lips. "Soldier, you saw the face of my daughter and for that you will die."

The drums rolled, the axe-man stepped forward and everyone held their breath. Suddenly, Jack saw the little boy running towards him, holding the tinderbox high.

Jack called out so loudly that everyone could hear. "Your Majesty," he begged, "please grant me one request before I die."

"What is it?" snapped the king impatiently.

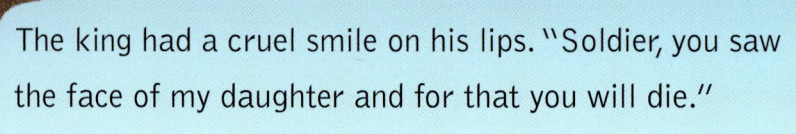

"Let me touch my old tinderbox once more," Jack pleaded. "The rusty thing was by my side during battles and dangers. Let me hold it now."

The crowd felt sorry for the soldier whose only crime was to meet the princess. "Grant him this last wish, Your Majesty!" they called.

"What harm can a tinderbox do?" snorted the queen.

The king nodded scornfully. "Untie the fool's hands and let him have his tinderbox. Much good may it do him!"

Chapter 8

As soon as Jack had the tinderbox in his grasp, he wished. Instantly, the first two dogs stood beside him, staring and glaring in the most terrifying way. Jack wished again and the third dog appeared, carrying the princess on its back. Everyone shrank with fear from those huge, cartwheel eyes.

However, the princess wasn't afraid. She jumped off, ran across to Jack and hugged him, smiling from ear to ear. How everyone cheered the soldier and princess – everyone except the king and queen.

"Seize him, men!" shouted the king.

"Beware!" Jack warned. "These hounds will do whatever I wish."

The great dogs growled, showing their sharp teeth, so the guards stepped back.

Jack raised his hand. "Listen!" he declared. "Your Majesties, you've treated your people badly for too long. Now it's time for the princess to rule this land instead."

"Hooray!" people called.

"I will," cried the princess, "but first I'll marry Soldier Jack and he'll rule beside me!"

Everyone cheered, including the captain of the guard and his men. They were glad to have a leader like Jack instead of the cruel, lazy king.

The king and queen had no choice. With the crowd still cheering for the new rulers, they left. Terrified of what the dogs would do if they hung about, they packed quickly, but as they tried to stuff as many treasures into their carriage as they could, the wheels shattered. So instead, they were forced to leave the palace with only the clothes on their backs. The three dogs stood at the gates, watching to make sure they left.

The next day, the wedding bells rang out and everyone was invited to a most magnificent feast. Jack sat there with the beautiful princess at his side, the three dogs at his feet and the tinderbox tucked safely in his pocket. And from that day on, so they say, the land was ruled wisely and well.

Ideas for reading

Written by Clare Dowdall, PhD
Lecturer and Primary Literacy Consultant

Reading objectives:
- increase familiarity with a wide range of books including fairy stories and retell orally
- identify themes and conventions
- discuss words and phrases that capture the reader's interest and imagination
- draw inferences and justify these with evidence

Spoken language objectives:
- participate in discussions, presentations, performances, role play, improvisations and debates

Curriculum Links: PSHE

Build a context for reading

- Read the title and explain what a tinderbox is if children are unfamiliar with this term (a box for storing fire-lighting material).
- Look at the illustrations on the front and back covers and read the blurb together. Ask children what they can deduce about the old woman from the information provided.
- Ask children to explain what a "favour" is. Discuss how they'd feel in Jack's position, if an old woman asked them to do a favour in return for money, and what they'd do.

Understand and apply reading strategies

- Read pp2–3 aloud to the children to introduce the story. Dwell on the phrase "meet good fortune" and discuss what it means. Ask children to think of moments of good fortune in their lives to help build connections between experience and the story.
- Ask children to read pp2–3 again to themselves, looking for words and phrases that give clues about the old woman's character and intentions. Ask them to share their ideas.